I0784058

Oscar

The Second Coming

Oscar
The Second Coming

A graphic novel written and illustrated by
Dan Pearce

an editions

AN Editions

aneditions.co.uk | editors@aneditions.co.uk

British Library Cataloguing in Publication Data
A catalogue record for this book is available from the British Library

ISBN 978-1-7384023-0-4

'It's delightful! Very, very funny … Anyone with a true sense of him should find it wholly engaging!'

—**Stephen Fry**

THE OLD BAILEY, 25th MAY 1895...
OSCAR WILDE; YOU HAVE BEEN FOUND GUILTY OF THE MOST HIDEOUS CRIMES...

THE SENTENCE OF THIS COURT IS THAT YOU BE IMPRISONED AND KEPT TO HARD LABOUR FOR TWO YEARS...
Oh my GOD

HISS
the SHAME of it... the HUMILIATION...
BOO!

READING GAOL, SEVERAL MONTHS LATER...
HM PRISON

I suppose I have no-one to blame but myself... and that deceitful worm BOSIE... I shall write him a letter...

MANY WEEKS LATER...
"your lack of imagination, your hatred, your greed..."
What the...?

What is this unearthly LIGHT? It seems to be drawing me...

up..?

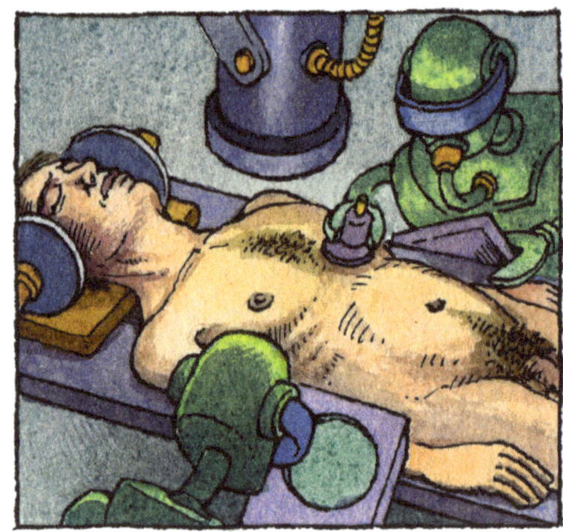

What a bizarre dream... but this is not my cell...
is it?

OI!
My God - I am not alone! And I am NAKED!

WHO THE FUCK ARE YOU?
I might ask you the same question...

HELP! THERE'S A NAKED PERVERT IN OUR CELL!
Please don't hit me - I mean no harm!
CHEEKY FUCKER

WHAT'S ALL THIS RACKET? WHO'S THIS? HOW DID HE GET IN?
SEARCH ME, HE'S SOME FUCKIN' NUTTER...
YEAH, GET HIM OUTTA HERE...

The prison seems strangely changed... they've painted it a charming shade of green...

WHO'S THIS?
DUNNO, SIR, HE WAS CAUSING A DISTURBANCE IN ONE OF THE CELLS — NAKED HE WAS, SIR...
REALLY? IS HE AN INMATE?

DON'T THINK SO, SIR — NOT ON MY WING, ANYWAY...
WHAT'S YOUR NAME?
WILDE, SIR — Oscar Wilde...
VERY FUNNY

WE'VE NO RECORD OF AN OSCAR WILDE...
THAT'S HARDLY SURPRISING...
But I have been imprisoned here for MONTHS!
INDEED? AND WHEN WERE YOU COMMITTED?

On the 21st of November, 1895, sir...
HA HA HA
DON'T BE ABSURD — THAT'S OVER ONE HUNDRED YEARS AGO!

This is either a nightmare or some cruel hoax designed to break my spirit — Have mercy on me, I beg you!

ENOUGH OF THIS NONSENSE. FIND HIM SOME CLOTHES AND LOCK HIM UP.
WHERE, SIR? ALL THE CELLS ARE FULL...
WELL PUT HIM BACK WHERE YOU FOUND HIM...

HE'S WITH YOU PERMANENT NOW, LADS — MAKE HIM WELCOME, WON'T YOU... HA HA HA
OH NO, NOT HIM AGAIN!
AT LEAST HE'S GOT SOME FUCKING CLOTHES ON...

Forgive me, dear boys, but I am confused... Tell me this is all a HORRIBLE DREAM...
THAT'S RIGHT...
THEY ALL SAY THAT WHEN THEY GET HERE...

Is this a newspaper? Where's the date... Oh my GOD... It's TRUE!

What am I going to do? (SOB) All my friends... My family (SNIFF) All DEAD... (SOB)

Tell me — Do I look one hundred and forty years old?

HERE, SEE FOR YOURSELF...
Thankyou... But — can this VISION be ME? I am rejuvenated!

And look at my TEETH — they're WHITE...
NEVER MIND YOUR FUCKING TEETH — WHO THE FUCK ARE YOU ANYWAY?
YEAH, AND HOW DID YOU GET INTO OUR CELL?

My name is Oscar Wilde. A name once renowned but now, alas, sadly besmirched by the so-called crimes that brought me here in the first place...
WHAT THE FUCK IS HE TALKING ABOUT?
SEARCH ME...

And as for this being YOUR cell, I must point out that I have prior claim to this cell...
YOU WHAT?

After all, I have been here since eighteen hundred and ninety five...
HE'S WEIRD...
HE'S A COMPLETE FUCKING LOONY...

MEANWHILE...

GOD KNOWS HOW HE GOT IN HERE BUT HE'S CLEARLY AS MAD AS A HATTER. WHAT ARE WE TO DO WITH HIM?
CAN'T WE JUST LOSE HIM... DUMP HIM SOMEWHERE?

TOO LATE FOR THAT, I'M AFRAID—TOO MANY PEOPLE KNOW ABOUT HIM. THE HOME SECRETARY WILL HAVE TO BE TOLD...
POOR SOD—AS IF HE DOESN'T HAVE ENOUGH ON HIS PLATE ALREADY...

...MY GOD...BUT THAT'S IMPOSSIBLE... THE SECURITY IMPLICATIONS...NO, NOT A WORD—WE DON'T WANT THE PAPERS TO GET HOLD OF IT...

NEXT MORNING...
OH SHIT!
NAKED MAN FOUND IN PRISON
HOW DID HE GET IN

WILDE! YOU'RE TO SEE THE DOCTOR...
Certainly, officer, just as soon as I've finished...
NOW!

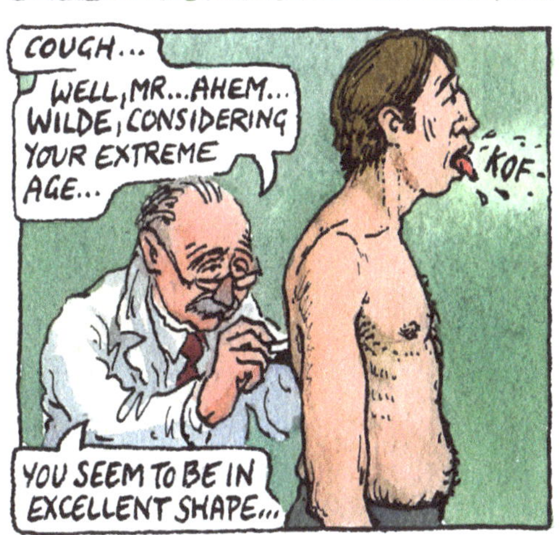

COUGH...
WELL, MR...AHEM... WILDE, CONSIDERING YOUR EXTREME AGE...
KOF.
YOU SEEM TO BE IN EXCELLENT SHAPE...

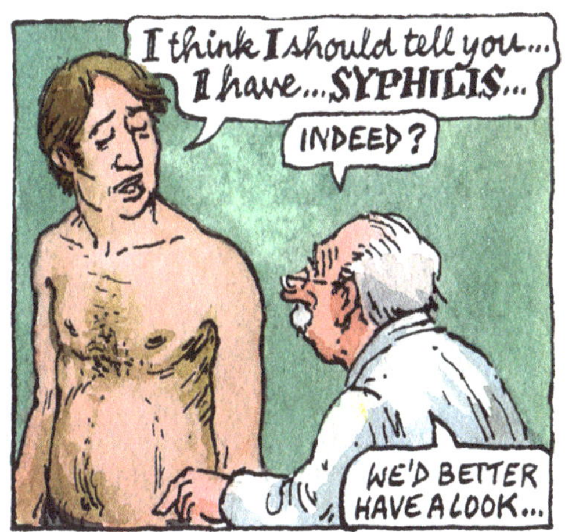

I think I should tell you... I have...SYPHILIS...
INDEED?
WE'D BETTER HAVE A LOOK...

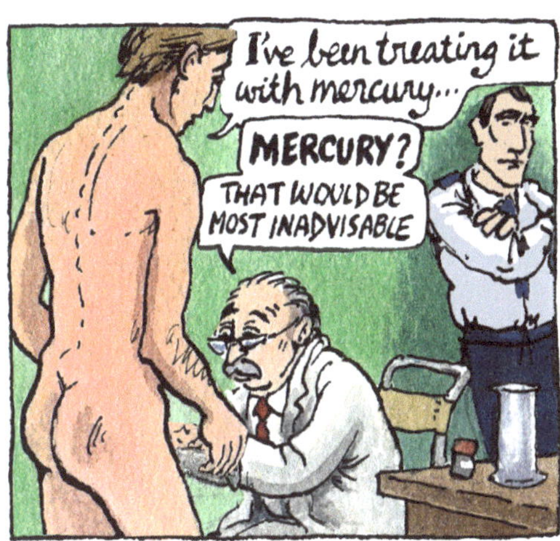

I've been treating it with mercury...
MERCURY?
THAT WOULD BE MOST INADVISABLE

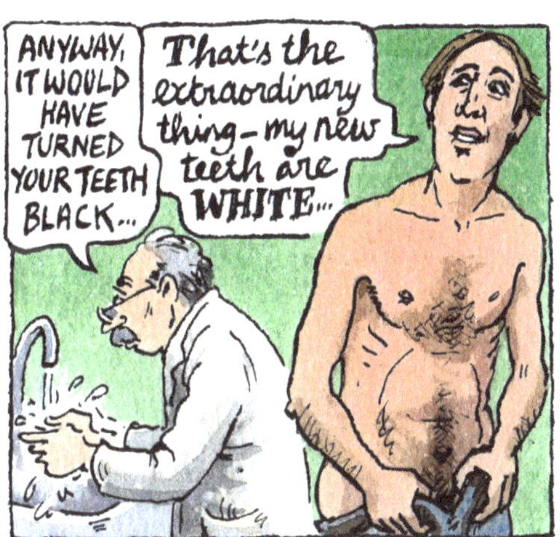

ANYWAY, IT WOULD HAVE TURNED YOUR TEETH BLACK...
That's the extraordinary thing—my new teeth are WHITE...

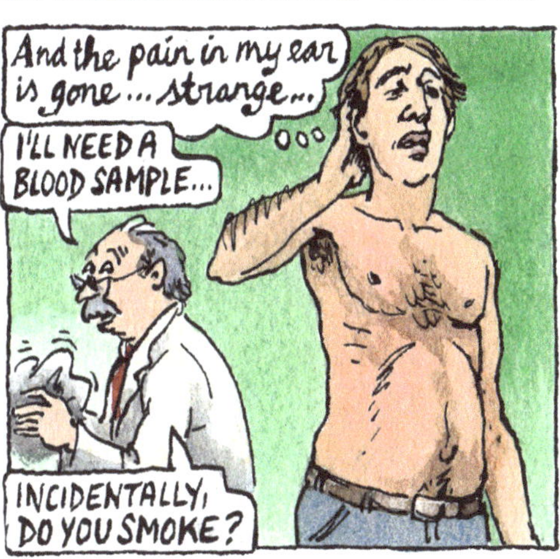

And the pain in my ear is gone...strange...
I'LL NEED A BLOOD SAMPLE...
INCIDENTALLY, DO YOU SMOKE?

I'm afraid not; I haven't smoked a cigarette since my incarceration... Of course I shall resume at the earliest opportunity... after taking a few lessons perhaps, in the MODERN style...

I SHALL ASSUME YOU ARE JOKING, MR WILDE ...NOW THIS WON'T HURT, IT'S JUST A LITTLE PRICK...
One must be grateful for small mercies...

YOU'RE TO SEE THE SHRINK NEXT...
What is a SHRINK?
THE TROUBLE WITH YOU, WILDE...
IS YOU ASK TOO MANY BLEEDING QUESTIONS!

I'M A PSYCHIATRIST MR WILDE, PLEASE SIT DOWN...
Aha! You study the psyche—How intriguing...

I have spent a lifetime exploring the mysteries of MY psyche... It is endlessly diverting and makes for such AMUSING conversation....

TELL ME ABOUT YOUR MOTHER...
SPERANZA... Oh mama...
They did not permit me to attend her FUNERAL!
YOU ARE CLOSE?

WHEN DID SHE DIE?
Barely a month ago she was fresh in her grave... But now...Oh God, NOW she is...mere BONES...

Oh the HORROR... (SOB) Forgive me (SNIFF)
YOUR CHILDHOOD WAS HAPPY?
HERE...

Oh yes... Of course Mama always longed for a daughter... Until the age of ten I was dressed as a girl...

I often played the fairy princess... We were always a very theatrical family...

Oh God— not again...
AND WHEN DID YOU DISCOVER THE ROLE OF OSCAR WILDE?

It's VERY simple. Mama named me Oscar Fingal O'Flahertie Wills Wilde in eighteen fifty-four and as far as I know I am still he... I mean, who else could I POSSIBLY be?

LATER... IT'S A MOST UNUSUAL CASE— HE APPEARS TO BE IN A STATE OF SHOCK FROM SOME RECENT TRAUMA... HIS MOTHER'S DEATH, PERHAPS...
MMM...

WE STILL HAVE NO IDEA HOW HE GOT IN— IT IS COMPLETELY BAFFLING...
MAYBE HYPNOSIS WOULD REVEAL SOMETHING?
CERTAINLY WORTH A TRY...

DID YOU KNOW THAT OUR MAN APPEARED IN THE SAME CELL THAT THE REAL OSCAR WILDE DISAPPEARED FROM ONE HUNDRED YEARS AGO?
WHAT AN EXTRAORDINARY COINCIDENCE...
POSSIBLY...

MEANWHILE... It is too vexing— they will not believe me...
YEAH—WELL I DON'T BELIEVE YOU...BUT IT'S A GOOD STORY...

HEY OSCAR—YOU MUST'VE DONE SOMETHING REALLY BAD TO GET A HUNDRED YEARS IN THE NICK...
Oh yes indeed...

My CRIME, Trevor, was to tell the TRUTH, to confront the English with their HYPOCRISY...
YOU WHAT?

That, and some minor indiscretions with certain BOYS...
!
SEE, I WAS RIGHT— HE'S A FUCKING GRISTLE-GRABBER!

YOU OLD PERVE – DID YOU DO IT WITH LITTLE BOYS?
CERTAINLY NOT— Boys of... your age...
HELP!
BUT THAT'S LEGAL!

My crime is no longer a crime? In that case I should be released IMMEDIATELY! I must speak to the governor!
WOZ HERE

I'M AFRAID THE MATTER IS OUT OF MY HANDS—YOU'LL HAVE TO WAIT FOR THE HOME SECRETARY TO MAKE A DECISION...
Oh GOD...
I suppose after one hundred years a few more days will make no difference...

MEANWHILE YOU HAVE BECOME A CELEBRITY— LOOK AT THESE NEWSPAPERS...
Indeed? How very gratifying...
But this is OUTRAGEOUS! They are calling me a LUNATIC!

I THINK YOU MIGHT FIND THIS STORY PARTICULARLY INTERESTING...
?
READING JOURNAL
UFO SEEN OVER READING
STRANGE LIGHTS IN SKY ABOVE PRISON
FLYING SAUCER!

LATER... IN THE HOUSE OF COMMONS TODAY THE HOME SECRETARY FACED QUESTIONS AFTER ADMITTING THAT A NAKED MAN HAD BROKEN INTO READING PRISON...
NEWS AT SIX
HEY
YEAH
THAT'S YOU, OSCAR!
Good heavens!

HAVE CONDITIONS UNDER THIS GOVERNMENT SUNK TO SUCH DEPTHS THAT PEOPLE ARE DRIVEN TO SEEK REFUGE IN OUR PRISONS?
HEAR HEAR!
They are talking about ME on this extraordinary kaleidoscope...
COR! YOU'RE FAMOUS!

WE ARE TAKING STEPS TO TIGHTEN SECURITY AND CERTAIN PRIVILEGES WILL BE WITHDRAWN. THE MAN IN QUESTION WILL BE CHARGED WITH ILLEGAL ENTRY...
SHAME!
Oh no! I don't BELIEVE it!
BAD LUCK, MATE!

LOOK AT HIM, THE BIG POSTURING PONCE...
HE'S VERY POPULAR.
WELL HE'S GETTING ON MY TITS...

I THINK YOU MIGHT HAVE TO GIVE HIM A SMACKING, BAZ.
HE SEEMS OK TO ME...
YEAH, FOR A POOF... HEE HEE!

LATER...
It is too frustrating... I despair of ever leaving this place...
HAVE A TOKE ON THIS — IT'LL DO YOU GOOD...

How kind — I think I might permit myself a moderate inhalation...
THIS GEAR IS THE DOG'S BOLLOCKS...
I BEG your pardon?

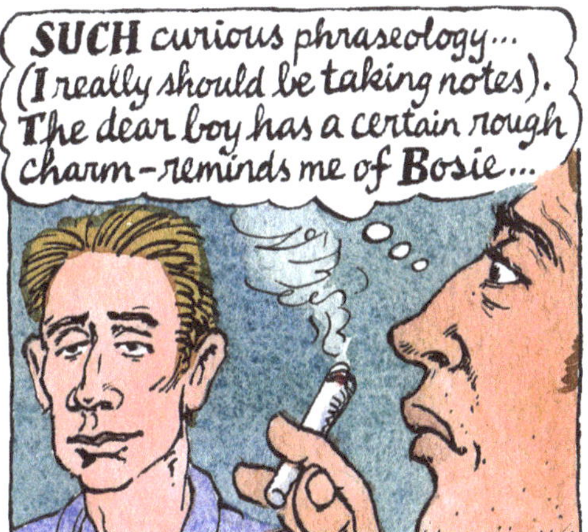

SUCH curious phraseology... (I really should be taking notes). The dear boy has a certain rough charm — reminds me of Bosie...

Ah Bosie... the times we had...

How he deceived me, the poisonous leech... how I LOVED him... and now he's gone, like all the others...

WHAT'S UP, OSCAR — ARE YOU CRYING?
Not at all, dear boy, the smoke got in my eyes...

NEXT DAY...
THIS IS MISS GOODWIN — SHE IS TO DEFEND YOU IN YOUR FORTHCOMING CASE...
HOW DO YOU DO...
You are a lawyer? Forgive me, but you are a WOMAN...

AND YOU, I GATHER, HAVE BEEN LIVING IN THE PAST. NOW, IF I AM TO REPRESENT YOU, I NEED THE FACTS. WHAT IS YOUR REAL NAME?
I am getting very tired of this interminable charade...

I realise the truth is fantastic but it is the truth, none the less...
SO YOU CLAIM YOU ARE OSCAR WILDE AND THAT YOU HAVE BEEN A PRISONER HERE FOR ONE HUNDRED YEARS? YOU EXPECT THE COURT TO BELIEVE THAT?

Of course, had I actually been incarcerated for so long I would by now be a loathsome cadaver instead of this thing of beauty you see before you...
OH VERY GOOD...

YOU REFER TO "THE PICTURE OF DORIAN GREY!" YOU HAVE CLEARLY DONE YOUR HOMEWORK...
And you are clearly a young lady of excellent education...

IF WE ARE TO WORK TOGETHER YOU CAN CUT OUT THE "YOUNG LADY" STUFF. NOW IS THERE ANYTHING YOU NEED?
Yes!
I crave contemporary literature. The novels here are pure dross...

WHAT A STRANGE MAN...SO CONVINCING I ALMOST BELIEVE HIM — BUT OF COURSE THAT'S ABSURD...
POLICE

HOW CAN I DEFEND HIM EXCEPT ON GROUNDS OF INSANITY?

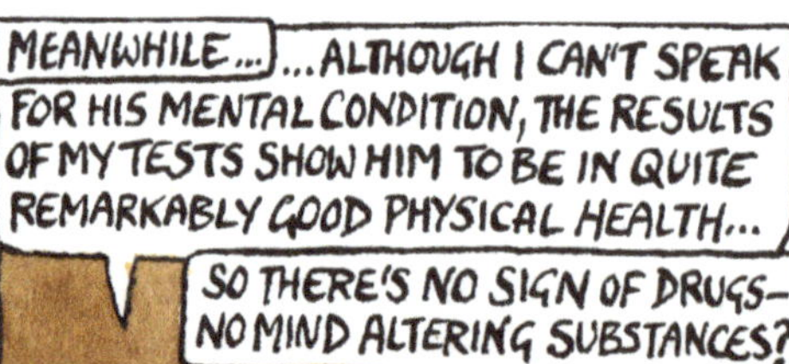
MEANWHILE... ...ALTHOUGH I CAN'T SPEAK FOR HIS MENTAL CONDITION, THE RESULTS OF MY TESTS SHOW HIM TO BE IN QUITE REMARKABLY GOOD PHYSICAL HEALTH...

SO THERE'S NO SIGN OF DRUGS— NO MIND ALTERING SUBSTANCES?

NO TRACE OF NARCOTICS, HALLUCINOGENS OR TOXINS OF ANY KIND — NO TRACE OF ANYTHING...IT'S MOST PECULIAR AND I DON'T UNDERSTAND IT...
NO, NEITHER DO I...DO EXCUSE ME, DOCTOR...
RING

HELLO?...YES...WHAT? ARE YOU SERIOUS? BUT IT'S GOT NOTHING TO DO WITH... BUT THERE'LL BE CHAOS... OH VERY WELL, THEN...GOODBYE!
THE BLOODY MAN'S GONE COMPLETELY ROUND THE BEND...

LATER... I am told that no home is without such a television device... I am undecided as to whether such a phenomenon is of cultural benefit or merely promotes mass narcosis...

But I have a particular fondness for this serialised drama – the visual effects are most lifelike although the dialogue is somewhat banal...
reminds me of Dickens...

and it is certainly very popular with the boys...
SORRY LADS...
CLICK
WHAT THE..?
OI!

NO MORE TELLY BY ORDER OF THE HOME SECRETARY...
I WAS WATCHING THAT!
WHAT THE FUCK?

AND IF YOU WANT TO KNOW WHY, YOU CAN ASK MISTER WILDE...
Oh GOD...

YOU! MISTER FUCKING WILDE! WHAT ARE YOU GOING TO DO ABOUT IT?
ME? Well...I do have many wonderful stories of my own...

I'm SURE you'd enjoy them...
I'M NOT LISTENING TO FAIRY STORIES FROM A FAT FUCKING FAGGOT!
I say...

Steady on!
I'M GONNA PUNCH YOUR FUCKING HEAD IN!

!
!
!
!
?

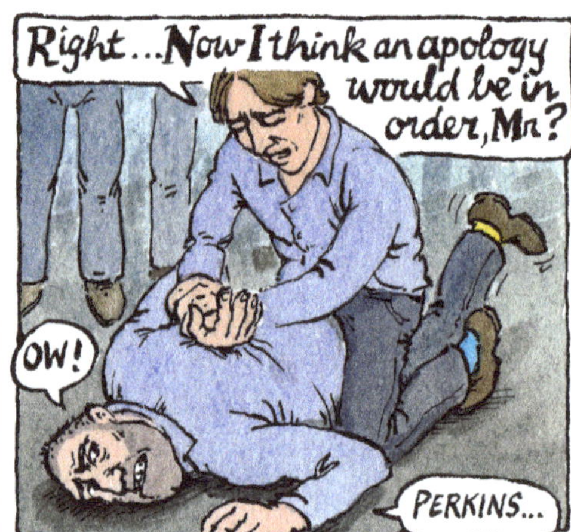
Right... Now I think an apology would be in order, Mr?
OW!
PERKINS...

Well, Mr Perkins?
I'M SORRY—I'M VERY SORRY FOR WHAT I SAID...SIR...

Very graciously put, I'm sure... Now perhaps you'd like to stay and listen to a most diverting tale I am about to tell you...
THANKYOU...
"SIR"! "THANKYOU"! WOW!

...concerning a very famous poet who found himself transported to another world by creatures from another planet...

LATER...
I EXPECT YOU'VE HAD NO END OF PROBLEMS SINCE THE T.V. BAN?
NO SIR, NOT AT ALL— MR WILDE HAS BEEN TELLING STORIES TO THE BOYS...
REALLY?

YES SIR, HE DOES A GOOD LINE IN FAIRY STORIES—HE'S GOT THEM EATING OUT OF HIS HAND...EVEN PERKINS!
CURIOUSER AND CURIOUSER...

I'VE GOT A LOT OF TIME FOR MR WILDE, SIR—HE'S A REAL GENTLEMAN...
YES, I AGREE...LET'S HOPE HE HAS SOME LUCK TOMORROW...

I HEARD ABOUT YOUR BUSINESS WITH MRS WILDE. MADE YOU LOOK A BIT OF A TIT, I GATHER...
HE BEAT ME, WHAT CAN I SAY?
AND NOW YOU KISS HIS ARSE...
I NEVER TOOK YOU FOR A PANSY...

CALL ME A PANSY AGAIN AND I'LL...
HE'S A GOOD BLOKE — YOU LEAVE HIM ALONE, OK?
RELAX! IT WAS A JOKE!

TOMORROW...
Today the curtain opens on a new act in this absurd farce...
JUST GET IN THE VAN, SUNSHINE...

...as once again I am taken to the courtroom to be charged with illegal entry to one of Her Majesty's prisons...

OH DO SHUT IT, WILDE...

HERE WE ARE... SHIT! REPORTERS!
QUICKLY NOW AND NO TALKING!
HEY!
OSCAR!
MR WILDE
Aha!

JUST A FEW WORDS, OSCAR!
WHAT ABOUT THE ALIENS?
HOW DID THEY GET IN?
WE SHOULD'VE PUT A BLANKET OVER HIS HEAD...

Good morning, Miss Goodwin, and how do you rate our chances?
I'M VERY OPTIMISTIC. JUST TELL THE TRUTH AND YOU'LL BE A FREE MAN BY TEATIME...

The TRUTH? In my experience it is invariably a mistake to confound the legal brain with the undiluted truth...
WE SHALL SEE... COME ON, WE'RE NEXT — GOOD LUCK!

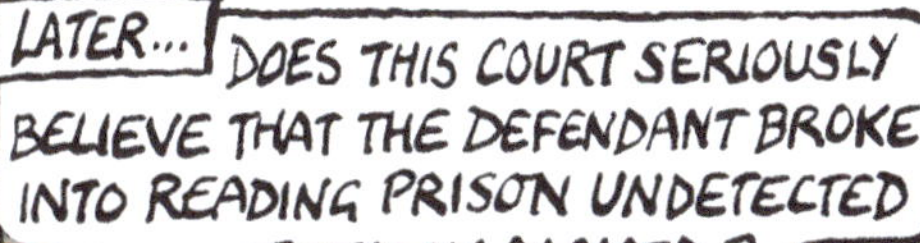

LATER...
DOES THIS COURT SERIOUSLY BELIEVE THAT THE DEFENDANT BROKE INTO READING PRISON UNDETECTED TOTALLY NAKED?

THE COURT WILL AGREE THAT IT IS LESS FANTASTIC THAN THE DEFENDANT'S CLAIM THAT HE IS NOT ONLY THE GENUINE OSCAR WILDE BUT THAT HE ALSO ARRIVED BY TIME TRAVEL...
HA HA

I WOULD LIKE THE DEFENDANT TO READ THIS — IT IS MOST RELEVANT TO THE CASE...
VERY WELL...
?

Aha — a poem... Would the court like a recitation?
NO! JUST READ IT TO YOURSELF...

I say, this is frightfully good — I could almost have written it myself...

SO THIS POEM IS UNKNOWN TO YOU?
Yes, but...

THANK YOU. THIS POEM, "THE BALLAD OF READING GAOL", WAS WRITTEN BY OSCAR WILDE ONE YEAR AFTER YOUR SO-CALLED ABDUCTION FROM READING PRISON...
OH!

PROVING CONCLUSIVELY THAT YOU ARE NOT THE REAL OSCAR WILDE...
I take your point — a bizarre paradox indeed...

I must congratulate you on a masterly peroration which...
SILENCE IN COURT!
SHUT UP, OSCAR!
THANK YOU...

THE DEFENDANT WILL KINDLY KEEP HIS OPINIONS TO HIMSELF. IN THE LIGHT OF HIS PREPOSTEROUS DEFENCE AND THE COMPELLING EVIDENCE AGAINST HIM, WE FIND HIM GUILTY AS CHARGED.
TAKE HIM AWAY...
Come now — It's not ALL bad...
OH GOD...

Amazing! This is obviously mine... So familiar... yet utterly strange...
A QUICK WORD, OSCAR?
NO PICTURES!

I BLAME MYSELF. HOW COULD HAVE I MISSED IT?
You weren't the only one... This is really VERY good stuff...
OH, FOR HEAVEN'S SAKE, OSCAR!
CANTEEN

DON'T YOU SEE? EITHER YOU'RE AN IMPOSTER, OR...
Yes, of course I see. I'd simply prefer not to think about it just now. It's giving me a headache...

YOU SAID YOUR LAST MEMORY WAS BEGINNING A LETTER TO BOSIE? MANY CONSIDER THAT LETTER RANKS AMONG YOUR FINEST WORKS...
What? A mere letter?
IT'S MORE THAN SEVENTY PAGES LONG...
Good Lord!

I was VERY cross with him at the time... Of course, I'm DYING to read it...
By the way, how do I die?

LATER...
ME AND THE LADS JUST WANNA SAY WE'RE SORRY AND THAT BUT WE'RE GLAD TO SEE YOU BACK, SIR...
I'm touched, Basil, but I can honestly say the pleasure is all yours...

Oh, and by the way, Hodges, thank you so much for the loan of the suit...
DON'T MENTION IT, MR WILDE—ANYTIME...

Oh God... Am I to endure this dingy and artless cell forever?

and when I think of my rooms at Oxford...

Boys! We are victims of cultural deprivation! We must beautify our surroundings, for without beauty the spirit will surely starve...
BEAUTY?

LOOK AT THE ARSE ON THAT, OSKIE — THAT'S FUCKING BEAUTY FOR YOU...
I grant you she has a certain charm, Derek, but not QUITE my cup of tea...

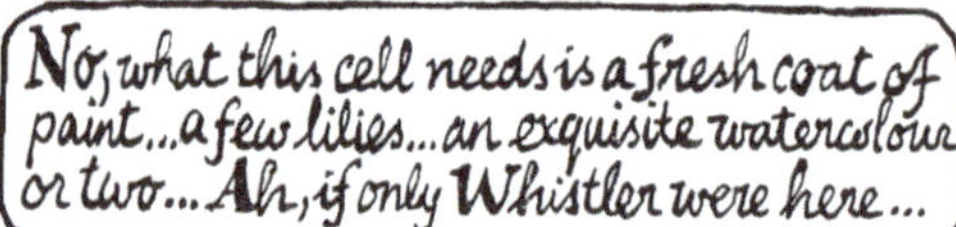

No, what this cell needs is a fresh coat of paint... a few lilies... an exquisite watercolour or two... Ah, if only Whistler were here...
WHO'S WHISTLER?
An old, dear friend... Must be VERY old by now...

NEXT DAY... THESE BOOKS CAME FOR YOU, MR WILDE, SIR... AND I GOT THE PAPERS...
Excellent! Very kind of you, Basil...

ME AND THE LADS ARE HAVING A WORKOUT IN THE GYM LATER — CARE TO JOIN US?
Good idea... But I cannot resist a glance at the newspapers...

Mmm... The usual English preoccupation with the female breast... Nothing changes... But what is this?

Quite fantastic... Pure invention...
HIS WILDEST DREAMS DASHED
SEX WITH SPACE MONKS
EXCLUSIVE! OSCAR — MY HEARTBREAK

The yellow press still peddles fiction but the reputable journals seem most sympathetic to my plight...
WHO BREAKS THIS BUTTERFLY ON THE WHEEL?
IS HE THE REAL THING?
RELEASE THIS MAN NOW

They weren't as kind to me one hundred years ago...
MR WILDE!

Ah... the heady perfume of raw masculinity...
So, Basil, what do you suggest?

I thought ordeal by treadmill had been abolished...
PUFF
PANT

LOVELY DEFINITION IN THE TRICEPS, IF YOU DON'T MIND ME SAYING SO...
Not at all, dear boy - please continue - I can stand any amount of immoderate praise...
May I introduce myself...

OH I KNOW WHO YOU ARE - I'M A BIG FAN OF YOUR WORK!
You've read me? Then you are unique in this prison... Also very charming... but you don't strike me as the athletic type...
OH, I WORK OUT... ACTUALLY, I GIVE MASSAGES...

I'M VERY GOOD... AND VERY REASONABLE...
Really? How fascinating...and how fortunate - thanks to a draughty cell I have a stiff neck... I don't suppose..?
I'D BE HONOURED...

BUT LADY BRACKNELL'S MY ABSOLUTE FAVOURITE... HOW'S THAT?
Mmm- much better...
You do have a lovely touch, Billy...

I say - that's not my neck...
I KNOW - THIS IS A LITTLE THANKYOU FOR LADY B AND ALL THE OTHERS...
Oh well, since you put it like that...

Well that grubby little cherub knows a thing or two... Oh God - how utterly sordid... How degrading...

How delightful...

THAT EVENING...
SO ARE YOU GOING TO TELL US A STORY, OSK?
I might later...maybe for one of Derek's exotic cigarettes..?
HUH - YOU'LL BE LUCKY...
SELECTED LETTERS OF OSCAR WILDE

But I've been thinking... Are either of you of an aesthetic bent?
No, no—I mean, do you have an artistic soul?
'ERE! YOU CALLING ME BENT?

Do you draw, paint?
I USED TO BE A SIGNWRITER...
YEAH, AND A CAR THIEF...
Oh, how intriguing—what's a car?

NEXT DAY... Hodges, dear chap—I'd like a word with the governor about an idea of mine...
YOU LEAVE IT TO ME, MR WILDE...

HE SAYS THE MEN SHOULD BE ENCOURAGED TO BEAUTIFY THEIR SURROUNDINGS...
OH MY GOD...
YOU CAN ALWAYS SAY NO, SIR...
YES, BUT IT'S NOT AS SIMPLE AS THAT—MY WIFE IS DESPERATE TO MEET HIM...

NEXT DAY... Boys—you'll never guess—the governor and his wife have invited me for tea! Can you believe it? What an accolade!
OH YEAH? THEY SAY SHE'S A BIT OF A GOER...
YEAH, BUT HE'S NOT INTO PUSSY...
COME ON, IT'S YOUR TURN...

But aren't you pleased for me?
LOOK, WE DON'T GIVE A TOSS WHAT HAPPENS TO YOU BUT IF YOU THINK THAT LICKING THE GOVERNOR'S ARSE IS GOING TO HELP THEN GOOD LUCK...

Oh... Well, thank you for being so frank, Derek... But you do believe I'm really me, don't you?
I DON'T KNOW WHO THE FUCK YOU ARE—I DON'T KNOW WHO THE FUCK OSCAR WILDE IS, ALL RIGHT?
YOU COULD BE MICKEY MOUSE FOR ALL I KNOW...

Now I even doubt myself... I know I was once Oscar but whether I am the same man today seems increasingly unlikely... and who on earth is Mickey Mouse?
KAFKA

But, my God, how I miss my dear, dead friends...

NEXT DAY... DON'T TAKE ANY NOTICE OF DEREK - HE GETS LIKE THAT WHEN HE'S OUT OF DOPE...
I sympathise with the poor boy...
What about you, Clive, do you believe me?

BELIEVE WHAT - FLYING SAUCERS? COME ON...
Quite absurd, I entirely agree... Anyway, my session of hypnotic therapy this afternoon may prove revealing...

Mmm, macaroni cheese - my favourite...
REALLY? YOU LIKE THIS SHIT?
It could be a lot worse...

Excuse me, do you mind if I..?
YES I FUCKING DO MIND - DON'T YOU QUEERS HAVE A TABLE OF YOUR OWN?
Yes, but...
WELL FUCK OFF THEN...

I'll go, but under protest. Your behaviour is appalling...
I'M SORRY, WHERE ARE MY MANNERS? PLEASE SIT DOWN...
What? Well thank you...

May I introduce my... Oh God - What have I sat in?

Ugh! Macaroni cheese - how revolting! But who..?
Oh, I see...

Hodges! What are you doing?
I SAW WHAT HE DID, THE LITTLE BASTARD...
But you're hurting him!
LEAVE THIS TO ME, SIR...
COME ON OSKY!

Hodges seemed to enjoy hurting that poor man for what was a childish prank...
WHAT DO YOU EXPECT? HE'S A SCREW...
Well, I'm deeply shocked - I shall have to speak to him about it...
YOU'RE CRAZY...

IT'LL DO NO GOOD—HE'S A FASCIST PIG...
What's a fascist?
OH... LATER, OSCAR
Yes—now I must go in search of clean trousers...

LATER...
TELL ME WHAT YOU SEE...
Light—incredible light!

Oh god—the claws! No! Don't touch me!
EXTRAORDINARY...

YES, INTERESTING CASE—COMPLETE NONSENSE, OF COURSE...
YOU THINK SO? BUT I THOUGHT YOU WERE SYMPATHETIC TO...
What are you doing to me?

LOOK—THE MAN'S MAD AND POSSIBLY DANGEROUS... YOU MUST BE CAREFUL!
OSCAR—DANGEROUS? YOU CAN'T BE SERIOUS...

NEVER MORE SERIOUS—THESE PEOPLE CAN BE VIOLENT, UNPREDICTABLE, IRRATIONAL...
BUT I CAN'T BELIEVE...

SUBJECT TO SUDDEN MOOD SWINGS...
BUT..!?

FOR GOD'S SAKE! WHY WON'T YOU LISTEN TO ME?
EXCUSE ME, SIR...
SIR?
AAH!

I'M ONLY TRYING TO PROTECT YOU!
GAK!

A FEW DAYS LATER...
What an idyllic spot... and such a convenient location...
YEAH. WATCH OUT FOR THE DOG - NASTY LITTLE BRUTE...
YAP YAP YAP

Delighted to meet you at last, dear lady...
MR WILDE! HOW SIMPLY THRILLING!
And your charming dog...

It's nothing, I assure you - barely broken the skin...
SUCH A NAUGHTY BOY, RAMBO!
I SEE YOU'VE MET THE DOG...
I'M SORRY...

No, allow me to commiserate on your most unfortunate altercation...
THANK YOU. I SUPPOSE THE WHOLE BLOODY PRISON KNOWS BY NOW...
HE SHOULD BE LOCKED UP... NOW DO COME THROUGH...
Why yes...

What an enCHANTING room - such EXQUISITE harmonies... Your touch, I guess, Mrs..?
HA HA! YOU GUESS RIGHT! AND PLEASE CALL ME MABEL...
GOOD GRIEF...

What a contrast to my cell... Thank you - a modicum of milk... (Sigh) Oh, the comforts of home...
I CAN IMAGINE... TEA?

Consider my fellow inmates - those poor men starved of visual stimuli - their aesthetic sensibilities dulled...
HMM...
OH, THOSE POOR MEN...

And I'd like to address this by giving an illustrated lecture and calling it "Cell Beautiful". What do you think?
SOUNDS WONDERFUL!
PLEASE EXCUSE ME - THE PHONE...

Oh dear - he didn't sound very enthusiastic...
DON'T WORRY, IT'LL ALL BE FINE. NOW THERE'S SOMETHING I'VE BEEN DYING TO ASK YOU...
Ask away, dear lady...

THE FLYING SAUCERS - THAT'S HOW YOU GOT HERE, RIGHT? IT IS TRUE, ISN'T IT? I KNEW IT! BUT THERE'S SOMETHING I STILL DON'T UNDERSTAND...
Ah, well - I'm really not sure about...

YOU WERE FIFTY-ONE WHEN YOU WERE SENT TO PRISON BUT YOU CERTAINLY DON'T LOOK THAT NOW - YOU'RE SO YOUNG AND SO FIT...
Mabel PLEASE - I'm a married man!
(Well at least I THINK I am...)

I cannot account for any of it, dear lady, but it is a great comfort to know that you believe me...
OH I DO! BUT HOW AWFUL TO BE LOCKED AWAY IN THIS FRIGHTFUL PLACE!

But it has its compensations and you, Mabel, are certainly one of them ...
OH OSCAR, YOU REALLY ARE A DEAR, DEAR MAN...

NEXT DAY...
YOU SAID YES?
I HAD NO ALTERNATIVE. MY WIFE IS VERY KEEN ON THE IDEA . I HOPE I HAVEN'T MADE A GHASTLY MISTAKE...

He said yes! But I think I have Mabel to thank...
WHY? DID YOU GIVE HER ONE?
Must you always be so coarse?

By the way, I found something very interesting in the pocket of Hodges' suit which proves he's not the villain you think he is, Trevor...
OH YEAH? WHAT'S THAT?

See this symbol on this invitation? It's an ancient Hindu sign of peace - It's called a swastika...
WHAT?
YOU ARE FUCKING JOKING...

Which proves that Hodges is clearly a member of some peaceful meditative cult - He's probably a Buddhist... Anyway, I must return his suit now - I'll see you boys later...
?

HE'S TOTALLY LOST HIS MARBLES...
YEAH, POOR SOD...
Oh, those poor, ignorant boys...

Thank you. Oh, and keep up the peace work. Well done!
I BEG YOUR PARDON?

Don't worry, your secret's safe with me...
Omm...
WHAT ON EARTH? IS HE ON DRUGS?

I don't know why but people are behaving very strangely today... Perhaps it's something I've said?

SOME TIME LATER...
SO HOW'S IT GOING?
The governor has approved my lecture – his wife is a great admirer of my work. Apart from that she has no taste at all...

Oh, I must tell you the latest gossip: Warder Hodges is a Buddhist!
I DON'T BELIEVE IT. DIDN'T YOU SAY HE WAS A SADISTIC THUG?
I know, but listen to this...

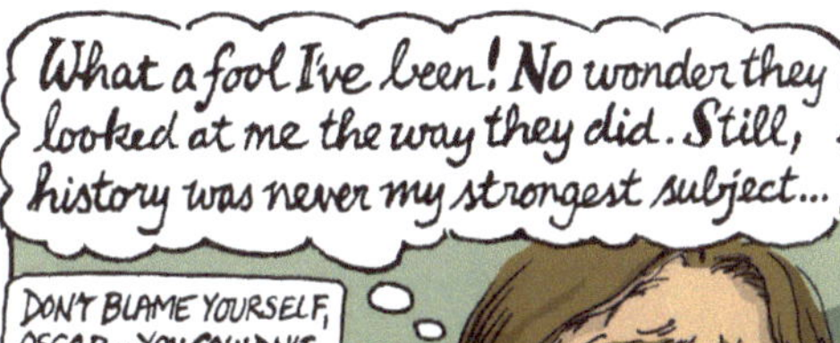

What a fool I've been! No wonder they looked at me the way they did. Still, history was never my strongest subject...
DON'T BLAME YOURSELF, OSCAR – YOU COULDN'T HAVE KNOWN...

Well boys, it seems I owe you an apology. Whatever Hodges may be, he's certainly no Buddhist...
YEAH – WE TOLD YOU THAT...
SO WHAT ARE WE GOING TO DO ABOUT IT?

Do you suppose I could try to persuade him to actually become a Buddhist? Oh. I'm sorry you think it's some sort of joke...
HA HA HA! BRILLIANT!
WHAT!?

LATER... What am I going to do with the wretched man? I'll have to speak to him. But what can I say?
AH, MR WILDE—JUST THE MAN I WANTED TO SEE...

THE GOVERNOR SAID TO SHOW YOU THE PROPS ROOM—SAID YOU WERE TO HELP YOURSELF...
Theatricals? I had no idea...
YEAH, THEY USUALLY DO A PANTO AT CHRISTMAS - YOUR SORT OF THING, I'D HAVE THOUGHT...

Pantomime? Certainly not. I leave such juvenilia to Gilbert and Sullivan. You won't have heard of them, of course...
OH YES—THEY DID "PIRATES OF PENZANCE" A COUPLE OF YEARS AGO...
How ghastly for you! you have my deepest sympathies...

But my dear Hodges, we really need to talk. There's been a misunderstanding and I fear it's entirely my fault...
OH YES?

The fact that you're a warder and I'm a prisoner makes what I have to say very difficult for me but you should know how I feel about your...

I THINK I KNOW WHAT YOU'RE TRYING TO SAY, MR WILDE...
You do?
I TOO HAVE FEELINGS BUT I'VE BEEN AFRAID TO SPEAK...
Really? But I don't...

OH SHUT UP AND KISS ME...
!?!

For heaven's sake!
PLEASE - PLEASE DON'T DENY ME YOUR LOVE!
What are you talking about?
BUT DON'T YOU WANT ME?
Well no, actually. I wanted to...

BUT I THOUGHT YOU...
OH GOD, DON'T YOU HAVE ANY FEELINGS FOR ME AT ALL?

I'm sorry, Hodges. I'm very flattered but I really wanted to talk to you about your membership of that vile fascist organisation...
OH. SO YOU KNOW...

Yes. I know. The boys know.
DOES THE GOVERNOR KNOW?
That rather depends on you.
I'LL DO ANYTHING...

Well, there are one or two things you could do...

NEXT DAY...
IT'S MOST IRREGULAR. THE CLASSES ARE MEANT FOR INMATES ONLY. HOWEVER, I'M PREPARED TO MAKE AN EXCEPTION IN YOUR CASE.
THANK YOU, SIR...

LATER... Knowing how keen your wife is on my forthcoming lecture, I wanted to ask her if she had any suitable fabrics she might lend me.
I'M SURE SHE HAS. I'LL ASK HER. INCIDENTALLY, HAVE YOU BEEN TALKING TO HODGES LATELY?

We do speak occasionally. And he's helping me with the set for my lecture. Any particular reason for asking?
NO. BUT HE HAS BEEN BEHAVING RATHER STRANGELY. HE WANTS TO TAKE UP YOGA...

Extraordinary. Oh, may I say how delighted I am to see you fully recovered from that brutal attack...
YOU MAY. THANK YOU. NOW I MUST ASK YOU TO DO SOMETHING FOR ME...

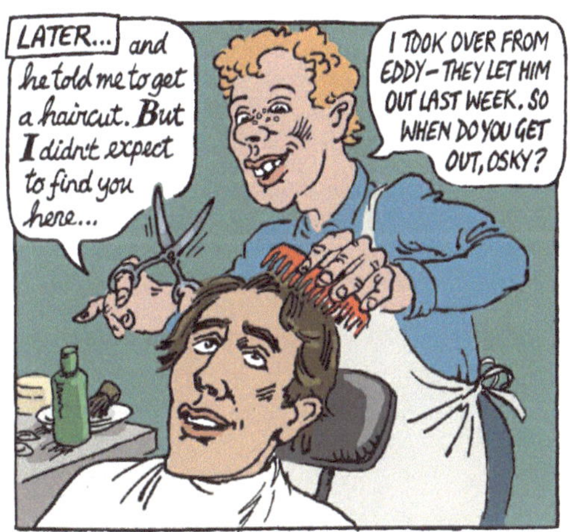

LATER... and he told me to get a haircut. But I didn't expect to find you here...
I TOOK OVER FROM EDDY - THEY LET HIM OUT LAST WEEK. SO WHEN DO YOU GET OUT, OSKY?

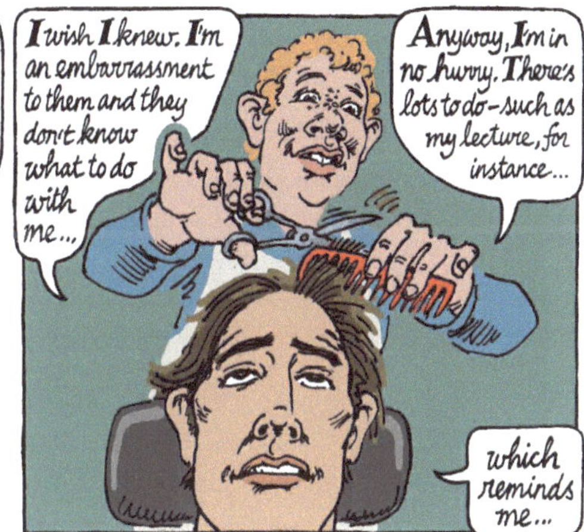

I wish I knew. I'm an embarrassment to them and they don't know what to do with me...
Anyway, I'm in no hurry. There's lots to do - such as my lecture, for instance...
which reminds me...

I need an artist to help design my set...
YOU DO? WELL I'M YOUR BOY!

Oh God, Billy, what have you done to me?
DON'T BE LIKE THAT— I'M JUST A BEGINNER. ANYWAY, I THINK YOU LOOK LOVELY...

This is a disaster. I shall have to postpone my lecture until my hair grows back...
Or wear a wig...

Go ahead, laugh... I'm so glad to be able to bring such amusement to your drab lives...
TEE HEE!
HA HA!

LATER...
This makes no sense at all... Oh god, another interminable night to get through...

But she'll be here in the morning and maybe she'll have some good news... And, please god, some decent literature...
MODERN CLASSICS
ULYSSES
JAMES JOYCE

Or am I to spend the rest of my life trapped in this stinking, airless cell?

NEXT MORNING...
What news of my appeal?
WHAT HAPPENED TO YOUR HAIR? ACTUALLY IT'S RATHER CUTE BUT IT DOES MAKE YOU LOOK LESS LIKE OSCAR WILDE...
What are you talking about?

LOOK AT THESE PHOTOS OF YOU...
But they were taken one hundred years ago when I was old and my cheekbones had disappeared. And the camera always failed to capture my essential beauty...

MAYBE. ALL I'M SAYING IS YOUR APPEAL WOULD STAND A BETTER CHANCE IF YOU LOOKED MORE LIKE YOU USED TO LOOK.
But what am I to do? I have been shorn of my crowning glory...

And sometimes I simply feel badly drawn...
WHAT NEWS OF HODGES? IS HE NOW A REFORMED CHARACTER?
I'm told he's taken up yoga...

But I'll believe it when I see it...
LOVELY TREE, MR HODGES!

I thought I had convinced her but I obviously didn't. Maybe she's right. Am I the same man or some alternative version of myself? Does the authentic version, coarse featured with black teeth, still languish in my old cell?
MARGARET ATWOOD
DORIS LESSING
TROPIC OF CANCER
EVELYN WAUGH
FEMALE EUNUCH
LAWRENCE DURRELL
Hmm... perhaps I should be writing this down...

NEXT DAY...
Please excuse my poor draughtsmanship but it should look something like this. What do you think?
NO PROBLEM, OSCAR...
LOOKS GOOD TO ME...

And you and Billy will paint the set...
OH YEAH? WELL I HOPE HE'S BETTER WITH A PAINTBRUSH THAN HE IS WITH A PAIR OF SCISSORS...
Amen to that...

MY WIFE HOPES THIS WILL BE OF SOME USE TO YOU...
How generous! Please tell her how grateful I am...
I WILL. AND YOU HAVE MY DEEPEST SYMPATHIES FOR YOUR HAIR CUT...

She's given me this hideous fabric and I can't think what to do with it...
WHAT ABOUT CURTAINS?

Maybe a Grecian influence? A pediment perhaps...
CELL BEAUTIFUL

But I feel the Corinthian style is much too fussy — I think we should go for Doric, don't you?
YOU TOOK THE WORDS RIGHT OUT OF MY MOUTH...

I want you to be my liaison officer, Hodges, here's a list of things I'm going to need...

AND HE WANTS FLOWERS! CAN YOU BELIEVE IT?
OH? AND WHY SHOULDN'T HE HAVE FLOWERS?

BECAUSE THIS IS A PRISON, NOT SOME HIPPY UTOPIAN REST HOME!
DON'T BE RIDICULOUS! OF COURSE HE CAN HAVE FLOWERS AND HE CAN HAVE MY MOTHER'S BLUE DELFT VASE TO PUT THEM IN...

I need a picture to hang on the wall. But where...?
MAYBE SOMEONE IN THE PAINTING CLASS?
Of course! Why didn't I think of that?

I was wondering where I could find a picture when inspiration hit me — your painting class!
COME AND HAVE A LOOK...
ART ROOM

I say! What a wealth of talent you have here!
WE LIKE TO THINK SO... DID YOU HAVE ANYTHING PARTICULAR IN MIND?

I don't know — a rural idyll, perhaps?
YOU'LL BE LUCKY... HEY, I KNOW WHO YOU ARE — "OSCAR WILDE", RIGHT?
Please do not address me in inverted commas, it makes me feel like a footnote...

WHAT ABOUT A PORTRAIT? MY CLASS COULD PAINT YOU — WE NEED PEOPLE TO SIT FOR US...
A portrait of ME?! What a wonderful idea!

And the first prize could be to take tea with me in our cell...
THAT SHOULD GET THEM GOING...
HERE'S THE POSTER – WHAT DO YOU THINK?

MR WILDE'S POSTER FOR YOUR APPROVAL, SIR...
WHAT'S THIS "PAINTING COMPETITION"? DO YOU KNOW ANYTHING ABOUT THIS?

THE TROUBLE WITH WILDE IS THAT HE'S NOT A CRIMINAL, HE'S JUST A BLOODY NUISANCE...

And I shall need invitations for the worthy citizens of Reading... And the local press of course...
OF COURSE...

I can't see how he could possibly object – after all, it would be such excellent publicity for the prison...
WILL HE NEVER STOP TALKING?

A WORD IN YOUR EAR, HODGES, IF YOU'RE NOT TOO BUSY RUNNING ERRANDS FOR MRS WILDE?

THE FEELING IS THAT YOU TWO ARE GETTING ON A BIT TOO WELL...
I'VE BEEN ORDERED TO HELP HIM. DO YOU THINK I ENJOY IT?
OF COURSE YOU DO. JUST KEEP US UP TO DATE, OK?

IT'S SO FRUSTRATING! AS GOVERNOR I CAN DO NOTHING. ON ONE HAND IS THE HOME SECRETARY AND ON THE OTHER IS MY WIFE!
HUH. HE THINKS HE'S GOT PROBLEMS...

I SEE... SO YOU'RE TELLING ME YOU HAVE NO IDEA HOW MUCH LONGER I HAVE TO PUT UP WITH HIM – A MAN WHO, ALTHOUGH PERHAPS MILDLY DELUDED, IS OTHERWISE ALMOST CERTAINLY INNOCENT...

TODAY WE'RE GOING TO PAINT MR WILDE'S PORTRAIT...
PLEASE, MISS, CAN'T WE PAINT HIM IN THE NUDE?
Hello!
YES, BILLY, BUT YOU MIGHT GET RATHER COLD...

SOME TIME LATER...
OH, NICE BIT OF CUBISM, PABLO...
YOU WHAT, MISS?
I feel like Whistler's mother sitting here...

I THINK THE EYES ARE A BIT TOO CLOSE TOGETHER... THE NOSE IS VERY GOOD THOUGH...
I do hope this hasn't been a big mistake...

LATER... BUT BILLY, HIS HAIR'S NOTHING LIKE THAT...
But it's the Oscar my admirers would recognise...
I KNOW— AND IT'S ALL MY FAULT...

Not that I blame you, Billy, but for my lecture I do need gravitas - I don't want to look like a Dickensian murderer...
YOU COULD WEAR A HAT?
I'M SURE I'VE SEEN A PORTRAIT OF LORD BYRON WEARING A TURBAN...

LATER...
Of course, Byron is one of my heroes...
YOU'LL LOOK FABULOUS...
A little higher... Oh that's perfect...

But what am I to wear? Although Hodges' suit fits me rather well, I can't wear it with a turban...
I COULD RUN YOU UP A TOGA...
THERE'S A NICE PAIR OF CURTAINS IN THE PROPS ROOM...

I should be swathed in the finest silks...
OH DO BE SERIOUS...
All right. But I will need a cloak...
OH. SO IT'S THE CURTAINS THEN...

MEANWHILE... WE NEED CLOSURE ON THE WILDE BUSINESS... YOU KNOW, THE BLOODY MAN WHO THINKS HE'S OSCAR WILDE... WHAT?... BUT WE CAN'T LET HIM ROT INDEFINITELY... YES, BUT THE PSYCHIATRIST WHO WROTE THAT REPORT IS NOW IN A HOSPITAL FOR THE CRIMINALLY INSANE...

It was during my tour of America – I was at the height of my fame... They were wild, ill educated boys and we got on extremely well...

I only hope this lot will be half as appreciative. Which I doubt... But how strange is this lack of confidence... Why should I, with all my past successes, be now beset by doubts? As someone* so wisely put it: "I was so much older then, I'm younger than that now."

*BOB DYLAN

How delightful! Everyone's talking about me!
SOON BE OUT NOW, OSKY!
FUCKING FAGGOT...

HE'S GETTING A LOT OF SYMPATHY. WILL YOU BE RECOMMENDING HIM FOR PAROLE?
WILL YOU PLEASE STOP TALKING ABOUT HIM! YOU'RE AS BAD AS MY WIFE!

WE CAN HOPE FOR YOUR EARLY RELEASE ON COMPASSIONATE GROUNDS AS YOU'RE CLEARLY NO DANGER TO THE PUBLIC.
Oh, surely a little bit of danger between consenting adults can do no harm?

MY INVITATION ARRIVED THIS MORNING - I'M SO LOOKING FORWARD TO IT!
So am I, but my costume is a problem...

I'd appreciate your opinion - a woman's point of view...
I'D BE DELIGHTED - SUCH A PRIVILEGE TO GET A SNEAK PREVIEW...

This is Basil, in charge of set production...
HELLO BOSS...
CELL BEAUTIFUL
And Trevor - lovely job, Trevor...

And this is the suit...
YES, I KNOW THE SUIT... AMUSINGLY RETRO, VERY BING CROSBY...
"Bing"?
I DON'T REALLY THINK SO...

YOU REALLY NEED SOMETHING MORE FLAMBOYANT...
SOMETHING LIKE THIS?
Oh my GOD...
Where did you find that? It's PERFECT...

Simply gorgeous...
THERE'S ALL KINDS OF STUFF IN THIS TRUNK... OH LOOK - DANCING GIRLS' COSTUMES!
YEAH - I WAS A DANCING GIRL IN THE CHRISTMAS PANTOMIME ONCE...

LATER...
I WAS YUM YUM — IN LOVE WITH NANKI-POO...
Oh no, not "The Mikado"!
?

WE WERE TO BE MARRIED...

WHAT THE FUCK WAS THAT ALL ABOUT?
BYE, LADS...
Oh nothing. Just be very thankful you haven't experienced the full horror of a Gilbert and Sullivan opera...

NEXT DAY...
THE GOVERNOR SAID TO TELL YOU THAT IF ANYTING HAPPENS TO IT, THE SMALLEST CHIP, HE'LL SEE THAT YOU GET ANOTHER SIX MONTHS INSIDE...

VERY INTERESTING, THANK YOU...
MUM
IT'S GIVEN ME AN IDEA...

That was lovely, Billy — I owe you five cigarettes, I think?
CERTAINLY NOT, OSCAR — THAT WAS AN ACT OF LOVE...
That's sweet of you...

I HAVE SOMETHING TO TELL YOU, OSCAR, I'M BEING RELEASED IN TWO WEEKS...
Freedom? I'm so happy for you — how I wish I could join you...

But what would I do? How would I live?
I COULD GET YOU A JOB. MY UNCLE SELLS CARS — HE COULD USE A WELL SPOKEN CHAP LIKE YOU...
But I barely know what a car IS...

Let alone sell one...
I DO LOVE YOU, OSCAR...
OI! YOU KNOW THE RULES — NO HOLDING HANDS!

YOU SHOULD KNOW BETTER, OSCAR...
Of course I should but sometimes the heart has priority...
ANYWAY, THE GOVERNOR WANTS TO SEE YOU...

THE BOY'S A SLUT...
The green eyed monster raises its head...
Why does he want to see me?

YOU'LL SOON FIND OUT. IN YOU GO, LOVER BOY...
AH, WILDE-COME IN...
Buddhism really seems to be working for you, doesn't it?

PLEASE SIT DOWN. I'M AFRAID I'VE GOT SOME BAD NEWS FOR YOU. CELL BEAUTIFUL CAN NOT GO AHEAD...
What?!
PLEASE EXCUSE ME...

HELLO? OH MABEL...WHAT?...THAT'S KIND OF YOU BUT... HE'S HERE NOW...NO, HIS TALK IS CANCELLED, THE PRISON INSPECTORS ARE PAYING US A SURPRISE VISIT AND I CAN'T AFFORD TO TAKE ANY RISKS...

WHAT? YOU CAN'T DO THAT! IS THIS GUTLESS WRETCH THE MAN I MARRIED? OSCAR'S THE BEST THING THAT'S HAPPENED TO THIS PLACE! THIS COULD PUT YOUR PRISON ON THE MAP!
NOW LISTEN VERY CAREFULLY...

I didn't know you smoked...
I DON'T...
She's a forceful woman...
LOOK HERE, FORGET WHAT I SAID BEFORE. CELL BEAUTIFUL IS ON— BUT NOTHING MUST GO WRONG, OK?

NOTHING. THERE MUST BE NO TROUBLE—DO I MAKE MYSELF CLEAR? I'M RELYING ON YOU.
OH YES, ONE OTHER THING—NOT A WORD ABOUT THE CONVERSATION WITH MY WIFE.

SORRY TO HEAR YOUR FIFTEEN MINUTES OF FAME HAS GONE DOWN THE DRAIN... (SNIGGER)
I think it's safe to assume that fame is an affliction you will never have to suffer...

GAVE HIM A BOLLOCKING, EH? GOOD OLD MABEL!
HE'S PUSSY WHIPPED, THE POOR BASTARD...
What is "pussy-whipped"?

IF YOU DON'T MIND ME SAYING SO, YOU DID THE RIGHT THING THERE, SIR — COULD HAVE CAUSED A LOT OF TROUBLE...
CANCELLING WILDE'S TALK, OF COURSE...
WHAT ARE YOU TALKING ABOUT, HODGES?

LATER...
WHAT'S UP, MR HODGES? YOU DON'T LOOK VERY HAPPY...
IT'S THIS FUCKING TALK. ARE YOU SURE IT'S SAFE?
RELAX, MR HODGES, IT'S ALL GOING TO WORK OUT TO OUR MUTUAL BENEFIT...

I'M SURE YOU'VE DONE THE RIGHT THING, MY DARLING — IT'S BOUND TO BE A GREAT SUCCESS! NOW EAT UP AND STOP WORRYING...

LATER...
WELL I'M CERTAINLY LOOKING FORWARD TO IT — I THINK IT'S GOING TO BE WILDELY EXCITING! HA HA HA!
OH GOD, I HOPE I DON'T LIVE TO REGRET THIS...

ALL RIGHT YOU LOT — LIGHTS OUT. AND KEEP YOUR BLOODY MOUTH SHUT, WILDE, AND YOUR FLY ZIPPED IF THAT'S AT ALL POSSIBLE...

JUST REMEMBER I'M WATCHING YOU, WILDE...
ONE STEP OUT OF LINE AND YOU'RE DEAD MEAT...
Hodges! Are you threatening me? How thrilling!

I don't think it was wise to make an enemy of Hodges...
WOW! WHAT'S HER PROBLEM?
SLAM

God knows I have few enough friends and most of them are criminals...
GOODNIGHT OSKY — YOUR BIG DAY TOMORROW...

I shall soon be released into an alien world where I will be utterly alone and of ambiguous identity...

Even I am not completely convinced that I am who I think I am...

What have I become? What will become of me? What happened to the master of the bon mot?

Is this primitive creature all that remains of the wit that launched a thousand epigrams?

Has this transformation cost me my intellect?

And yet things aren't so bad...
There's something to be said for being young and beautiful...

The prison gymnasium — A long way from The Theatre Royal..
HI OSCAR! NEARLY FINISHED...

But maybe not so far from The Royal Academy. Some of these are rather good...
OSCAR! I'VE GOT SOMETHING FOR YOU...

YOUR TURBAN— WHAT DO YOU THINK?
Fabulous!
THE SET'S DONE— SEE YOU LATER...

MEANWHILE...
I'LL SEE YOU'RE NOT DISTURBED BUT BE QUICK ABOUT IT, OK?
CHEERS, MR HODGES - THE BOSS'LL BE WELL PLEASED...

ALL THESE CARS... WHAT..? OH, THE MEN FROM THE MINISTRY, OF COURSE... THAT VERY FAT MAN LOOKS FAMILIAR... IT'S THE HOME SECRETARY! OH MY GOD...

A GREAT HONOUR, SIR...BUT WHAT..?
WHAT AM I DOING HERE? WELL I'VE HEARD SO MUCH ABOUT YOUR SO-CALLED MR WILDE I THOUGHT I'D PAY YOU A VISIT. HIS TALK IS THIS AFTERNOON, IS IT NOT?
IT IS. BUT HOW DID YOU KNOW?
OUR SPIES ARE EVERYWHERE, HA HA...

NOW WE'RE ALONE I CAN TELL YOU THE REAL REASON I'M HERE. WE'RE LETTING WILDE GO. HE'S LANGUISHED LONG ENOUGH AT HER MAJESTY'S EXPENSE...
I'M DELIGHTED!

I SHALL MAKE THE ANNOUNCEMENT, LIVE ON TV, AT THE END OF HIS TALK. UNTIL THEN NOT A WORD TO ANYONE...

OK, THAT'S SORTED. BUKOWSKI'S IN PLACE.
GOOD. LET'S HOPE HE DOESN'T GET CRAMP...
OH, BY THE WAY, HAVE YOU HEARD ABOUT OUR MOST DISTINGUISHED VISITOR?

BLOODY HELL! WE'D BETTER CALL IT OFF...
WHY? IT MEANS THAT WILDE WILL END UP IN DEEPER SHIT...
OH, RIGHT...

AREN'T YOU EATING, OSCAR?
Much as I adore macaroni cheese, I never lecture on a full stomach...

Anyway, my dresser is waiting for me...
MACARONI CHEESE - YUCK!
OK, SEE YOU ON STAGE. GOOD LUCK!

20 MINUTES LATER...
Really, Billy, I look like some ghastly pantomime dame...
DON'T BE SILLY, YOU LOOK FAB!
NOW FOR THE TURBAN...

YOU KNOW THE HOME SECRETARY'S HERE? HE'S GOING TO FREE OSCAR - ISN'T IT WONDERFUL? BUT IT'S A SURPRISE, BASIL, SO YOU MUSTN'T SAY ANYTHING...
NOT A WORD, AND THANKS FOR THE FLOWERS, MRS...

HE'S CERTAINLY CHANGED OVER THE LAST HUNDRED YEARS - YOU'D HARDLY RECOGNISE HIM!
HA HA HA! VERY GOOD, MINISTER!

HELLO OSKY... GOR BLIMEY, LOOK AT YOU!
Please don't laugh, Basil...
SORRY. I GOT YOUR FLOWERS - SHE SAID THEY WERE YOUR FAVOURITES...
But I HATE chrysanthemums! And they're entirely the wrong shade of pink...
CELL BEAUTIFUL

TOO LATE TO CHANGE THEM NOW, OSC, YOU'RE ON IN A MINUTE...

YOU READY TO GO, WILDE?
As ready as I'll ever be...
This absurd charade will soon be over...
LET 'EM IN, MR HODGES!
CELL BEAUTIFUL

YOU MUST TELL ME ALL THE GOSSIP... DINNER TONIGHT?
AHA! MUST CHECK MY DIARY...

FASCINATING MAN - OF COURSE WE'RE VERY GOOD FRIENDS...
I'D LIKE TO MEET HIM...

What am I doing in this fancy dress?
I shall be a laughing stock...
LADIES AND GENTLEMEN! YOUR ATTENTION PLEASE...

AS GOVERNOR OF THIS ESTABLISHMENT, I'M PLEASED TO INTRODUCE ONE OF OUR MORE POPULAR AND CONTROVERSIAL, ER, GUESTS...

Loss of freedom is surely punishment enough! But although our surroundings are depressing, the fatal ugliness is inside us—

Negative emotions: anger, hate, envy...

Contemplation of beautiful things can soothe the inner demons and transport one to a place of serenity...
OW! I MUST HAVE DROPPED OFF...
OH FUCK, THAT'S THE SIGNAL!

Humble decor, enhanced by a solitary, exquisite object of beauty, such as this precious vase...
AAAH! MY VASE!!!

Aha... Sabotage! But who..?

Your vase, dear lady— safer in your hands, I think. Many apologies for the interruption.
MY HERO!

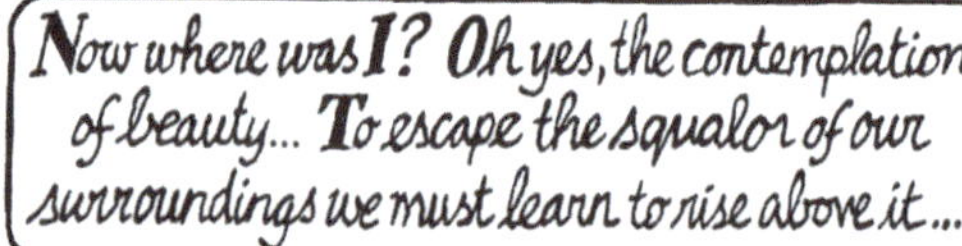

Now where was I? Oh yes, the contemplation of beauty... To escape the squalor of our surroundings we must learn to rise above it...

To fly on the wings of beauty to a place of peace...
What the...!?

WHGSWb35G...GSShr?
?sGPrce...
GG5G53!?!
GH57GR 35G1h! blb5!!
F5G...

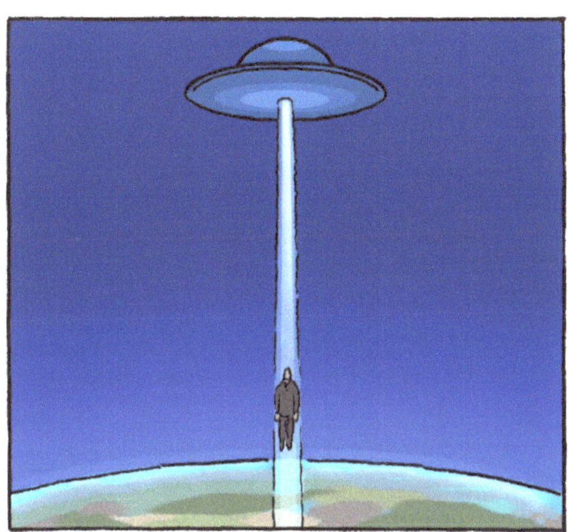

Oh yes, I was writing to Bosie... But why was I so cross with him? Perhaps I won't send it...
But it is so beautifully written...

The sun is up — I must have slept for hours... For the first time in months...

Such strange dreams... now slipping away... I can remember only fragments...

I do feel wonderfully well...
and my ear — the pain has gone!
CLKK CLUNK
GRUB'S UP!

AND HOW ARE WE THIS MORNING, MR WILDE?
Unusually well, thank you.
I feel like quite a different man...

I'M VERY GLAD TO HEAR...
!?!?

AN Editions, London | aneditions.co.uk | editors@aneditions.co.uk | arsnotoria.com